big NATE

THUNKA, THUNKA, THUNKA

More

adventures from

LINCOLN PEIRCE

Big Nate From the Top

Big Nate Out Loud

Big Nate and Friends

Big Nate Makes the Grade

Big Nate All Work and No Play

Big Nate: Game On!

Big Nate: I Can't Take It!

Big Nate: Great Minds Think Alike

Big Nate: The Crowd Goes Wild!

Big Nate's Greatest Hits

Big Nate: Say Good-bye to Dork City

Big Nate: Welcome to My World

big NATE

THUNKA, THUNKA, THUNKA

by LINCOLN PEIRCE

Andrews McMeel Publishing®

a division of Andrews McMeel Universal

YOU'RE A CELEBRITY.

ALL OVER TOWN, YOU'RE KNOWN AS "THAT GUY WHO HANDS OUT LAME HALLOWEEN CANDY."

YOU'RE FAMOUS FOR BEING A **LAUGHING-STOCK!** YOU'RE LIKE... LIKE...

THAT'S THE FIRST TIME IN MY LIFE I'VE EVER BEEN COMPARED TO CHARLIE SHEEN.
peirce

I WONDER HOW LONG I CAN MAKE MY HALLOWEEN CANDY LAST!

I ALWAYS TRY TO MAKE MINE LAST UNTIL NOVEMBER.
HUH? YOU MEAN DECEMBER.

BELCH!!

WHOO! PARDON MY MILK DUDS!
HE MEANS NOVEMBER.
PEIRCE

MY DAD IS A TOTAL HYPOCRITE.
HOW SO?

HE MAKES SUCH A BIG DEAL ABOUT HANDING OUT HEALTHY TREATS FOR HALLOWEEN!

BUT WHY DOES THAT MAKE HIM A HYPOCRITE?
IT DOESN'T. STEALING CANDY FROM MY STASH DOES.

STEP AWAY FROM THE PUMPKIN, DAD!
WHA-? WHO, ME?
Peirce

I'VE ALREADY EATEN ALL MY **GOOD** HALLOWEEN CANDY. ALL THAT'S LEFT IS THE DREGS.
CHOMP
CHOMP

YUCK. I DON'T EVEN **LIKE** THIS STUFF.
THEN DON'T **EAT** IT! THROW IT **AWAY!**
MUNCH
MUNCH

WHAT? THIS IS **CANDY**, FRANCIS! WHAT KIND OF **MORON** THROWS AWAY **CANDY**?

FIVE MINUTES LATER...
OOOOH...
LET'S TALK ABOUT MORONS AGAIN.
Peirce

NOW THAT I'VE EATEN ALL MY HALLOWEEN CANDY, TEDDY, I'M RANKING ALL OF 'EM FROM BEST TO WORST!

WHICH WAS THE MOST MEMORABLE? WHICH CANDY WILL ENDURE AFTER ALL THE OTHERS HAVE FADED AWAY?

...AND THE ANSWER, OF COURSE, IS "SUGAR BABIES."
Peirce

THTILL GOT THOME THTUCK IM MY TEETH, THEE?
THIS IS WHY I PREFER "SNO-CAPS."

JACKPOT! I THOUGHT I'D EATEN ALL MY HALLOWEEN CANDY, BUT THEN I FOUND ONE LAST **JUNIOR MINT!**

NUMF! NUMF!
NUMF! NUMF! NUMF!

WHERE WAS IT?
ON THE FLOOR UNDER MY BED!

JACKPOT, INDEED.
AND YOU'RE ALWAYS TELL-ING ME TO **VACUUM!**
Peirce

YOU'RE THE NICKNAME GUY, RIGHT?
YUP! I THINK UP ALL THE BEST NICK-NAMES!

WELL, I NEED A NICKNAME. I **HATE** MY NAME.
WHAT IS IT?

TIM. THERE ARE **TEN** OTHER TIMS IN THE SCHOOL.
OKAY, LET ME SEE WHAT I CAN DO.

I DON'T USUALLY INVENT NICKNAMES ON DEMAND, BUT GIVE ME A SEC. MAYBE SOMETHING WILL COME TO ME.

HMMMMM...

YOUR NICKNAME IS "ZIP."
"ZIP"! I **LIKE** IT!

...AND IT'S SO MUCH BETTER THAN TIM! **"ZIP"!** HA HA! THANKS A LOT!

SOMEBODY'S HAPPY!
SOMEBODY'S FLY WAS OPEN.

YOUR NEXT PROJECT WILL BE CONDUCTING AN INTERVIEW WITH A SENIOR CITIZEN!

WHAT'S THAT?
AN ELDERLY PERSON.

HOW OLD DO THEY HAVE TO BE?
LET'S SAY... SEVENTY.

WHAT IF SHE'S SEVENTY-FIVE BUT TELLS EVERY-ONE SHE'S SIXTY-SIX?
THAT'S FINE, CHAD.
Peirce

WHO ARE YOU GUYS GOING TO INTERVIEW FOR THE "SENIOR CITIZENS" PROJECT?
I HAVE NO IDEA.

WE HAVE TO INTERVIEW SOMEONE IN **PERSON**, AND MY GRANDPARENTS LIVE IN FLORIDA.
HEY, WHAT ABOUT MRS. BENBOW?

MRS. BENBOW ISN'T **SEVENTY**, FOOL!
SHE'S NOT? SHE **LOOKS** SEVENTY!

SHE'S FORTY-EIGHT.
YIKES.
I THINK BEING A LUNCH LADY IS A JOB THAT AGES YOU.
Peirce

HI GRAM!
WELL, **HI** SWEETIE! WHAT'S COOKIN'?

I HAVE TO INTER-VIEW A SENIOR CITIZEN FOR A SCHOOL PROJECT.
WHAT **FUN**!

WHO'S HAD A MORE INTERESTING LIFE: YOU OR GRAMPS?
WELL, LET'S SEE...

I'LL LET YOU DECIDE.
EH?
WHEEL! OF! FORTUNE!
Peirce

SO THIS IS A CLASS PROJECT, EH?
RIGHT. I HAVE TO ASK YOU QUESTIONS ABOUT YOUR LIFE.

GOTCHA! LET 'ER RIP!
OKAY... UM... WHERE WERE YOU BORN?

I WAS BORN ON A TRAMP STEAMER, SON, IN THE MIDDLE OF THE WORST TYPHOON IN...
OH, FOR HEAVEN'S SAKE.

YOU WERE BORN IN CLEVE-LAND.
MARGE, DO YOU WANT THE BOY TO GET A GOOD GRADE OR **NOT**?

OKAY GRAMPS, NEXT QUESTION: WHAT DO YOU REMEMBER MOST ABOUT YOUR CHILD-HOOD?
WORK, M'BOY! WORK!

MY DAD ALWAYS HAD CHORES FOR ME TO DO! CHOPPING WOOD! SHOVELING SNOW! WEEDING THE GARDEN!

I TELL YOU, I WAS ONE HARD-WORKING KID! I'VE **ALWAYS** BEEN HARD-WORKING!
Peirce

...AND YET, SOMEHOW, HE CAN'T MANAGE TO PICK HIS BOXERS UP OFF THE FLOOR.
YES, MARGE.

SO WHEN DID YOU AND GRAM GET TO-GETHER, GRAMPS?
WAY BACK! WE WERE HIGH SCHOOL SWEETIES!

OH HO! WAS IT LOVE AT FIRST SIGHT?
FOR ME IT WAS. NOT FOR HER.

BUT I WORE HER DOWN!
Peirce

HE'S STILL WEARING ME DOWN!
EXACTLY! I HAVEN'T LOST A THING!

SECOND AND GOAL FROM THE SEVEN-YARD LINE...
BRRRINNG!

HEY, TEDDY, WHAT'S UP?

YOU **ARE**? HEH HEH! LUCKY **YOU**! SOUNDS LIKE **FUN**!

ME? OH, I'M JUST HANGING OUT AT MY GRANDPARENTS' HOUSE, WATCHING THE GAME AND HAVING A BAG OF CHIPS!

WELL, LISTEN, DON'T LET ME KEEP YOU! BACK TO WORK! TRY NOT TO GET TOO MANY BLISTERS!
HA HA HA

CHUCKLE! TEDDY'S DAD IS MAKING HIM RAKE THE YARD!
HM.

THAT REMINDS ME OF SOMETHING.
OH, YEAH? WHAT?

HARDY HAR **HAR**.
Peirce

CAN I ASK YOU SOME QUESTIONS FOR MY SCHOOL PROJECT, GRAM?
SURE, HON. BUT WEREN'T YOU TALK-ING TO GRAMPS?

YEAH, BUT... THE INTERVIEW SORT OF SLOWED DOWN.

DID HE FALL ASLEEP?
NO, HE TURNED ON "JUDGE JUDY."

HE LIKES HER.
THEN **I** FELL ASLEEP.
PEIRCE

YOU GREW UP ON A DAIRY FARM, RIGHT, GRAM?
YUP! I LOVED THOSE COWS!

...AND THE GOATS AND PIGS AND CHICKENS, TOO! I'VE ALWAYS BEEN THE TYPE TO TAKE CARE OF CRITTERS!

THEN WHY DON'T YOU HAVE ANY PETS?
Peirce

MARGE, I LOST A BUTTON.
I CAN ONLY TAKE SO MUCH.

SO YOU REALLY WENT TO A ONE-ROOM SCHOOL-HOUSE?
I SURE DID!

DID ALL THE TEACHERS **SHARE** THE ROOM, OR...?
THERE WAS ONLY **ONE** TEACHER, SWEETIE! FOR FIRST GRADE TO EIGHTH!

IT WAS... WELL, IT WOULD BE LIKE **YOU** HAVING MRS. GODFREY AS A TEACHER FOR EIGHT YEARS!

FIVE MINUTES LATER...
I'M... STILL C-C-COLD...
I'LL MAKE US SOME COCOA!
Peirce

I THINK WE'RE DONE! THANKS FOR HELPING ME WITH MY INTER-VIEW, GRAM AND GRAMPS!
YOU'RE WELCOME, HON!

EH? WHAT'S THIS ABOUT AN INTERVIEW?
OH, HEY, UNCLE TED. IT'S JUST A SCHOOL PROJECT.
GNUT

WELL, MAY I ASK WHY I WASN'T INCLUDED?

BECAUSE YOU WERE BUSY WITH YOUR LITTLE COMPUTER GAMES.
IT'S CALLED "WORLD OF WARCRAFT," MOTHER.
GNUT
Peirce

SORRY, UNCLE TED. YOU CAN'T BE PART OF MY SCHOOL PROJECT.
BUT WHY **NOT**?
ZAGNUT

BECAUSE I'M INTER-VIEWING **SENIOR CITIZENS**! YOU HAVE TO BE OVER **SEVENTY**!

WELL, I MAY BE YOUTHFUL, MY BOY, BUT I'M AN **OLD SOUL**!
ZAGNUT
Peirce

AN OLD SOUL WHO CAN'T DO HIS OWN LAUNDRY?
MOTHER, I'M SIMPLY HELPING YOU FEEL **USEFUL**!

HERE'S MY "SENIOR CITIZEN" REPORT, MS. CLARKE!
THANK YOU, NATE! WHO DID YOU INTER-VIEW?

MY GRANDPARENTS! **BOTH** OF THEM! SO I INTERVIEWED **TWICE** AS MANY PEOPLE AS YOU ASKED US TO!

...AND IF THAT'S NOT ENOUGH TO GET ME EXTRA CREDIT, CHECK OUT WHAT'S ON THE LAST PAGE!

I INCLUDED GRAM'S RECIPE FOR MOLASSES CRINKLES.
Peirce

EVENS! I PICK FIRST!

I'LL TAKE FRANCIS!

CHAD.

JENNY.

JEFF.

ARTUR.

...AND I'LL TAKE SHEILA! LOOKS LIKE THE LAST PICK'S YOURS, TEDDY!
UH...

NO, THAT'S OKAY. YOU CAN HAVE HIM.
WHAT?

I DON'T WANT HIM!
WELL, NEITHER DO I!

TOUGH! HE'S YOURS!
NO, YOU TAKE HIM!
MAYBE I'LL JUST GO INSIDE AND WATCH FOOTBALL.
Peirce

UH-OH. HERE COMES MARCUS.
UGH.

HE'LL PROBABLY HAVE A BRAND NEW **INSULT** FOR US!

LOSERS.

...OR MAYBE HE'LL STICK TO THE CLASSICS.
STALE, BUT EFFECTIVE.
Peirce

I WISH I WERE BETTER AT COMING UP WITH SNAPPY COMEBACKS!

WHEN MARCUS CALLS US LOSERS, I WISH I COULD ANSWER RIGHT AWAY WITH A RAZOR-SHARP ZINGER!
HOW ABOUT "NINNY"?

IT'S INSULTING AND IT'S FUN TO SAY!

NINNY NINNY NINNY
NINNY NINNY NINNY
NINNY NINNY NINNY
NINNY NINNY NINNY
NINNY
CRIPES.
Peirce

OKAY, HERE COMES MARCUS! WHEN HE INSULTS ME, I'VE GOT THE **PERFECT** COMEBACK LOCKED AND LOADED!

FOILED AGAIN.
? WHA...? SPUTTER! OH, COME **ON!**
Peirce

HEY, **I'VE** GOT AN IDEA! NEXT TIME MARCUS INSULTS YOU, JUST **YO MAMA** HIM!
YOU CAN'T "JUST YO MAMA" PEOPLE, FRANCIS!

YOU ONLY DO IT DURING A "YO MAMA SMACKDOWN"! YOU DON'T YO MAMA PEOPLE AT **RANDOM**!

HOW WOULD YOU FEEL IF, OUT OF NOWHERE, I SAID TO YOU: "YO MAMA'S SO FAT, HER THIGHS ARE WHERE CORDUROY GOES TO DIE"?

UM... BAD.
EXACTLY! SEE, I'D NEVER **DO** THAT!
Peirce

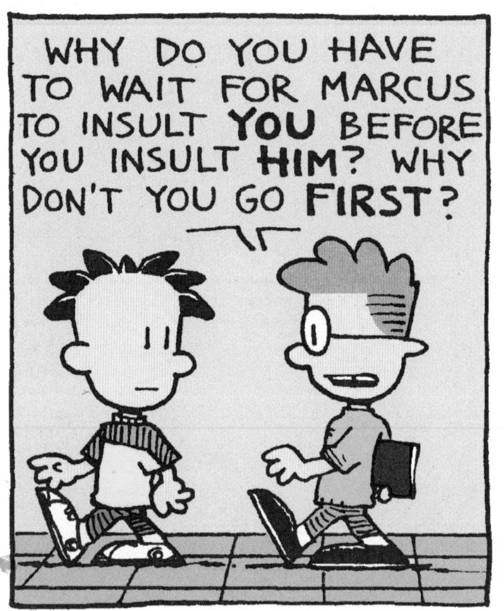
WHY DO YOU HAVE TO WAIT FOR MARCUS TO INSULT **YOU** BEFORE YOU INSULT **HIM**? WHY DON'T YOU GO **FIRST**?

FRANCIS, IF I JUST WALK UP TO MARCUS AND INSULT HIM, HE'LL **CLOCK** ME!

...BUT IF I COME UP WITH A WELL-TIMED, WITTY COMEBACK, **I'LL** BE THE GUY WHO PUT THE BULLY IN HIS **PLACE!** I'LL BE A **HERO!**

I'LL GET A STANDING OVATION... GIRLS WILL ADORE ME... THE YEAR-BOOK WILL
SOMEONE'S BEEN WATCHING TOO MANY TV MOVIES.
Peirce

HERE COMES MARCUS AGAIN! THIS TIME I'VE GOT THE ULTIMATE COMEBACK READY TO GO!

WHAT ARE YOU LOOKIN' AT, WUSSY FACE?
HEH HEH HAW!

I CHOKED.
...BUT ON THE BRIGHT SIDE, YOU MIGHT HAVE A FUTURE AS A MIME!
Peirce

LET'S PLAY PING PONG.
IN A SEC, TEDDY. I WANT TO WATCH THE WEATHER.

THE **WEATHER**?
I NEED TO SEE HOW WINK SUMMERS IS DOING.

EVER SINCE HE GOT DEMOTED TO WEEKENDS, HE'S **CHANGED!** HE HAS NO SPARK! NO ENERGY! HE'S JUST... **BLAH!**

I KEEP HOPING I'LL SEE THE **REAL** WINK AGAIN!
...AND NOW THE WEATHER WITH **WINK SUMMERS!**

UH... WINK?
WHAT?

THE WEATHER.

WHAT ABOUT IT?
LET'S PLAY PING PONG.
Peirce

AWRIGHT, SCRUBS! GET THE LEAD OUT!
COACH JOHN!
WHERE'S COACH CALHOUN?

AT A "PROFESSIONAL DEVELOPMENT CONFERENCE."
WHAT'S THAT?

THAT'S WHERE GYM TEACHERS FIND OUT ALL THE THINGS WE CAN'T DO IN GYM ANYMORE!

LIKE WIND SPRINTS, HEH HEH?
DREAM ON. LINE UP.

WE HAVE A **PROB-LEM** HERE, TROOPS! YOU'RE NOT RE-SPONDING TO MY **WHISTLE**!

WHEN I BLOW THE WHISTLE, I WANT TO SEE YOU **RESPOND**!

TWEEET!!

WRONG RESPONSE, CHAD.
I WANT TO GO HOME.

YOU URCHINS HAVE NO IDEA HOW EASY YOU HAVE IT!

WHEN I WAS YOUR AGE, MY COACH MADE US RUN 'TIL WE PASSED OUT!

COMPARED TO THAT, WHAT I'M ASKING YOU TO DO IS A CAKEWALK!

WE GET CAKE?
CHAD! SSH!
P.S. 38
Peirce

COACH JOHN SORT OF SCARES ME.
WHY DON'T YOU TRY TALKING TO HIM?

TALKING TO HIM? ABOUT WHAT?
ANYTHING! MAYBE IT'LL LOOSEN HIM UP IF YOU JUST... Y'KNOW... STRIKE UP A CONVERSATION!

UM... HI, COACH JOHN!... UH... REMEMBER AT JUNIOR LIFESAVING LAST SUMMER, WHEN NATE ACCIDENTALLY PULLED OFF YOUR TOUPEÉ?

RUN!!
IF WE'RE STILL ALIVE AFTER THIS, CHAD, I'M GOING TO KILL YOU.

COACH! YOU'RE BACK! HOW WAS THE CONFERENCE?
GREAT!

THE TOPIC WAS: "PUTTING THE FUN BACK IN PHYSICAL EDUCATION"!

LET'S GO, LADIES! SPRINTS AREN'T OVER!

THAT "FUN" THING: CAN WE START NOW?
PLEASE?

WOW, COACH! ARE WE EVER GLAD TO SEE YOU!
WELL, THANKS, BOYS!

WATER BREAK??

YOU DON'T NEED NO STINKIN' WATER BREAK!

DID WE MENTION HOW GLAD WE ARE TO SEE YOU?
WE'RE ECSTATIC.
Peirce

"LOCKERPALOOZA"? WHAT'S THAT?
A ONE-OF-A-KIND ENTERTAINMENT EXPERIENCE, THAT'S WHAT!
Locker-PALOOZA $2

FOR ONLY TWO BUCKS, YOU SPEND 5 MINUTES IN MY LOCKER!

WHAT? THAT'S THE STUPIDEST THING I...
HANG ON A SEC.
TIME'S UP, CHAD!
NOK NOK!

! !
'KAY!

THANKS, NATE! THAT WAS A BLAST!

HERE'S FIVE BUCKS! LEMME IN THERE!

KLIK!

FOOOM!

? ?
♪

WOW! SPITSY! YOU LOOK GREAT! YOU MUST HAVE A HOT DATE!

YOU DOG! WHO'S THE LUCKY GAL?
WURF!

THIS IS SO WRONG.
WURF
MYOW
ROWR
WURF
URF
MYOO
HEE
HEE
Peirce

SPITSY, WHAT IS **WRONG** WITH YOU? YOU CAN'T HAVE A **CAT** FOR A GIRLFRIEND! DOGS AND CATS ARE **ENEMIES**!!

WELL? SPEAK UP! WHAT DO YOU HAVE TO SAY FOR YOURSELF?

MYOW!

MYOW?
HEE HEE
I CAN'T TAKE IT.
MYOW MYOW!
HEE HEE
MYOW!
MYOW MYOW MYOW!
HEE HEE
Peirce

FRANCIS! HAVE YOU SEEN THIS?
SEEN WHAT?

SPITSY IS HAVING SOME KIND OF **ROMANCE** WITH YOUR STUPID **CAT**!

SPITSY... AND PICKLES?
YES!

THAT'S ADORA-
NO IT'S NOT!
Peirce

YOU'RE NOT UPSET ABOUT THIS?
UPSET ABOUT WHAT?

ABOUT SPITSY AND PICKLES, FRANCIS! DOGS AND CATS SHOULDN'T...
HEY, WHAT'S THAT ON HER PAW?

IT'S A RING!

THEY'RE ENGAGED!
SMAK!
PEIRCE

THIS IS RIDICULOUS! A DOG AND A CAT CAN'T BE ENGAGED!
I THINK IT'S CUTE!

MAYBE THEY'LL HAVE A FAMILY!
A FAMILY?

YEAH! THEY'LL HAVE LITTLE CATDOGS!
GREAT. CATDOGS...

...WEARING GOOFY COLLARS AND LICKING THEMSELVES!
WURF?
SLURP
SLUP
SLOP
SLUP
Peirce

SPITSY, THINK ABOUT WHAT YOU'RE DOING! GETTING ENGAGED TO PICKLES IS A PRETTY BIG STEP! HOW WELL DO YOU REALLY **KNOW** HER?

WHAT IF YOU'RE ALL WRONG FOR EACH OTHER? DOESN'T IT MAKE SENSE TO SLOW DOWN, TRY DATING SOME DOGS, AND...

...AND...

THIS MIGHT BE THE STUPIDEST CONVERSATION I'VE EVER HAD.
PANT
PANT
PANT
PANT
PANT
PANT
PANT

THIS STINKS.
WHAT DOES?

IT'S DECEMBER! IT SHOULD BE COLD! THERE SHOULD BE SNOW ON THE GROUND!
WELL... IT'S KINDA COLD.

IT'S WINDY, ANYWAY.
WIND, SHMIND! I WANT SOME WINTER WEATHER! NOW!

BUT IT ISN'T WINTER YET.
FRANCIS! LOOK!

SNOWFLAKES! IT'S STARTING TO SNOW!

I'M GONNA CATCH ONE IN MY MOUTH!
GNULP!

ACK! KOFF! PTOO! HOCK!

HACK! HOCK! KAFF KOFF!
GREAT DAY FOR GRILLING!
Peirce

YOUR SISTER GAVE ME HER CHRISTMAS WISH LIST. THERE ARE ONLY TWO ITEMS ON HERE YOU CAN AFFORD.
YEAH? WHAT?

YOU COULD BUY HER THE NEW "BETHANY" TREASURY...
"BETHANY"? THE WORLD'S LAMEST COMIC STRIP?

NO WAY! I REFUSE TO SPEND MY HARD-EARNED MONEY ON THE SO-CALLED "HEARTWARMING" ADVENTURES OF A TEENAGE AIRHEAD!

...OR YOU COULD BUY HER SOME "ME SO SASSY" UNDERWEAR.
HELLO, BOOK-STORE.
Peirce

HAVING TROUBLE FINDING SOMETHING?
UH, NO, THAT'S OKAY.

OH, LET ME HELP YOU! WE'RE REORGANIZING THE STORE, AND EVERYTHING'S ALL WILLY-NILLY!
IT'S...UM... *KOFF!* IT'S CALLED "BETHANY."

AH, THE **COMIC STRIP!** WE **USED** TO SHELVE THOSE TREASURIES IN THE "HUMOR" SECTION, BUT NO MORE!
Peirce

TO THE TEEN ROMANCE AISLE!
CRIPES.
EW!

HERE YOU ARE! THE LATEST "BETHANY" TREASURY: "NOBODY UNDERSTANDS ME."
THANK YOU.

UGH. WHY DID ELLEN ASK FOR **THIS** FOR CHRISTMAS? THIS COMIC STRIP IS SO **STUPID!** IT'S...

IT'S...

NEW
PHY
Peirce

WHAT A WASTE OF PAPER! WHO WANTS TO READ ABOUT THE LOVE LIFE OF SOME DOPEY HIGH SCHOOL SOPHOMORE?

PLUS, BETHANY IS SUCH A **DITZ!** WHY DOES SHE KEEP GOING OUT WITH **JASON**? ANY IDIOT CAN SEE THAT **EVAN** IS THE GUY FOR HER!

OH, **HERE'S** A SHOCK! JASON JUST **DUMPED** HER! LIKE WE DIDN'T SEE **THAT** COMING FROM A MILE A-

HEY!
GAH!

FRANCIS! WHAT ARE **YOU** DOING HERE?
WE'RE IN A **BOOKSTORE**, GENIUS! I'M LOOKING FOR A **BOOK**!

THE QUESTION IS, WHAT ARE **YOU** DOING IN THE "TEEN ROMANCE" SECTION?
NOTHING!
ZIP!

WHAT ARE YOU READING?
WHAT? I... KOFF!... I'M NOT READING THIS! I'M NOT READING **ANYTHING**!
ZING!

BONK!
Peirce

YOUNG MAN, WE DON'T **THROW** THINGS HERE AT THE BOOK LOFT!
S-SORRY. IT... UH... SLIPPED OUT OF MY HAND.

WELL, WHEN IT "SLIPPED," THE **COVER** WAS TORN! YOU'LL HAVE TO BUY THIS!
'KAY.

SNICKER!... YOU'RE BUYING A "**BETHANY**" TREASURY?
IT'S FOR MY **SISTER**!

THEN WHY WERE **YOU** SITTING ON THE FLOOR **READING** IT WHEN I FOUND YOU?
I HATE MYSELF.
KA-CHING!
Peirce

TEDDY! WHAT HAPPENED TO YOUR HEAD?
I WAS PLAYING STREET HOCKEY, AND I GOT WHACKED IN THE FACE.

I GOT TWO STITCHES! WANNA SEE?
OOH! YEAH!
NO. NO. NO.

I GET LIGHT-HEADED WHEN I SEE BLOOD. I MIGHT PASS OUT!
WHAT? OH, BROTHER!

SO YOU **FAINT** WHEN YOU SEE A **BOO-BOO**? FRANCIS, THAT IS THE **WUSSIEST** THING I'VE EVER HEARD!

WHAT ABOUT A **BLISTER**? DO YOU GET ALL DIZZY WHEN YOU SEE A...
OOPS. SORRY. I GOT FOOD ON YOU.

YOU... HUH?... WHAT IS THAT?
EGG SALAD.

EGG SALAD...

CLUNK!

HUH. MY BAD. THIS IS **CHICKEN** SALAD.

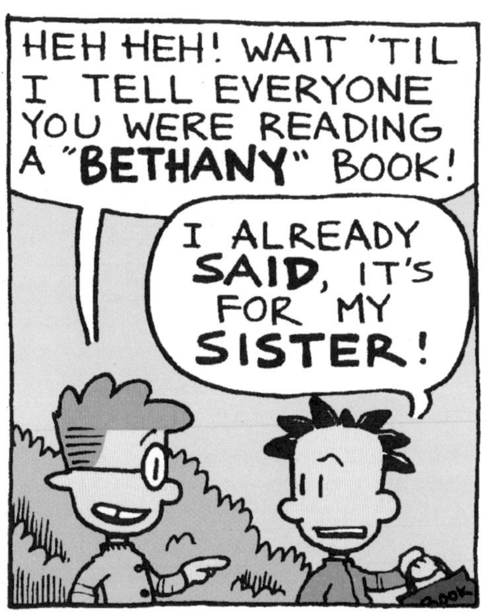
HEH HEH! WAIT 'TIL I TELL EVERYONE YOU WERE READING A "BETHANY" BOOK!
I ALREADY SAID, IT'S FOR MY SISTER!
BOOK

...AND YOU'RE NOT GOING TO TELL ANYBODY ABOUT IT, FRANCIS.
OH? WHY NOT?
BOOK LOFT

BECAUSE IF YOU DO, I'LL TELL EVERYONE SOMETHING ONLY I KNOW ABOUT YOU.
BOOK

LET US NOT SPEAK OF THIS AGAIN.
GOOD MOVE.
PEIRCE

YOU'RE NOT STILL PLANNING TO GIVE THAT BOOK TO YOUR SISTER FOR CHRISTMAS, I HOPE.
WHY NOT?

BECAUSE THE **COVER IS TORN**, THAT'S WHY NOT!
SO? IT'S NOTHING A LITTLE TAPE WON'T FIX!

SPLOOSH!

IT'S HARD FOR TAPE TO STICK TO WET SURFACES.
OH, COME ON!
PEIRCE

NATE, YOU DEFINITELY CAN'T GIVE YOUR SISTER THAT BOOK **NOW**!
HANG ON, FRANCIS! LET'S NOT BE HASTY!
DRIP DRIP

SURE, IT'S A LITTLE MOIST, BUT IF I PUT IT ON TOP OF THE RADIATOR IN MY BEDROOM, IT'LL DRY RIGHT OUT!
Bethany
NOBODY

GROWF!

MAYBE YOU SHOULD HAVE GONE WITH A GIFT CARD.
GRFF!
RRIP!
RIP!
GNRRRF!
Peirce

YOU'RE BACK! DID YOU GET THAT BOOK FOR ELLEN?
UH-HUH.

CAN I SEE IT?
UH...THEY WRAPPED IT AT THE STORE.
WELL, CAN I LOOK AT THE WRAPPING PAPER?
I...UM...

ARE ALL THESE NOSY QUESTIONS REALLY IN THE CHRISTMAS SPIRIT?!
BOOK

NICELY DONE.
HE DIDN'T NOTICE THAT THE BAG'S DRIPPING, SO I THINK I'M GOOD.
BOOK

THIS STUPID BOOK ISN'T DRYING FAST ENOUGH ON THE RADIATOR.
HOW ABOUT A HAIR DRYER?

HEY, DAD, DO YOU KNOW WHERE THE...?
WAIT A MINUTE.

CHUCKLE! WHAT AM I ASKING **YOU** FOR?
HEH HEH
PAT PAT!

HA HA HA HA HA HA
PEOPLE WHO LOVE THE SOUND OF CHILDREN'S LAUGHTER HAVE NO CHILDREN.

A COUPLE MORE PIECES OF TAPE, AND... **VOILÀ!**

GOOD AS NEW! YOU CAN BARELY TELL THE BOOK WAS RIPPED!
ARE YOU SERIOUS?

YOU'RE ACTUALLY GOING TO WRAP THAT THING UP AND GIVE IT TO YOUR **SISTER**?
HM. I SEE YOUR POINT.

THIS IS THE UGLIEST WRAPPING PAPER I'VE EVER SEEN.

HI, MR. EUSTIS!
WELL, WHAT HAVE WE HERE? CAROLERS?

YUP! WHAT DO YOU WANT TO HEAR?
I'LL LET YOU DECIDE!

OKAY, GUYS! LET'S DO OUR SPECIALTY!
HUMMM...

SLEIGH BELLS RINNNG... ARE YOU LISTENIN'... IN THE LAAANE... SNOW IS GLISTENIN'...

A BEAUTIFUL SIGHT... WE'RE HAPPY TONIGHT...

BOOM CHICKA BOOM CHICKA BAPPITY BAPPITY BABA BOOM!

THAT'S NOT EXACTLY HOW I REMEMBER "WINTER WONDERLAND."
WAIT 'TIL YOU HEAR ME ON "LITTLE DRUMMER BOY"!
Enslave the
Peirce

MERRY CHRISTMAS, ELLEN!
OOH, THE NEW "BETHANY" TREASURY!... WAIT... WHAT THE...?

WHY IS IT WARPED?
IT... UH... WAS THE LAST COPY THEY HAD, SO...

IT'S ALL RIPPED UP! AND TAPED BACK TOGETHER!
KOFF! ... WHICH DOESN'T DETRACT AT ALL FROM...

ARE THESE TEETH MARKS?
THIS MIGHT BE A GOOD TIME TO GET SOME FRESH AIR.
Peirce

NICE **GIFT**, NATE! YOU EXPECT ME TO **READ** THIS?
WHY NOT? IT'S A LITTLE BEAT UP, BUT...

A LITTLE BEAT UP? THERE ARE **PAGES MISSING**!
WHAT?

HOW'D **THAT** HAPPEN? I WAS SURE I TAPED IT ALL BACK TO-GETHER... WHERE'D THOSE PAGES GO?

HEE
HEE
HEE
HEE HEE
Peirce

MY DAD CHEWED ME OUT FOR GIVING ELLEN THIS BEAT UP BOOK FOR CHRISTMAS.
WELL, IT SERVES YOU RIGHT!

WHAT? IT WASN'T **MY** FAULT THAT IT GOT WET, AND SPITSY CHEWED IT UP, AND...
BUT IT ALL STARTED WHEN YOU THREW IT AT THAT CLERK IN THE BOOK STORE!

BOOKS ARE TO **READ**, NOT TO **HIT** PEOPLE WITH!

DOOF!
Peirce

HIYA, SPITSY. WHAT DID YOU GET FOR CHRISTMAS?
SPITSY

A BALL OF YARN? OH, COME ON! THAT'S A GIFT FOR A CAT!

I KNOW YOU LIKE CATS AND EVERYTHING, BUT THAT DOESN'T MEAN YOU HAVE TO START ACTING LIKE ONE! YOU DON'T... UM...

OH.
KNIT
KNIT
KNIT
KNIT
KNIT
KNIT
KNIT
KNIT
Peirce

SPITSY, THAT'S THE SAME SWEATER YOU **ALWAYS** WEAR.
WURF!

WHEN I SAW YOU YESTERDAY, YOU WERE KNITTING A **NEW** SWEATER.

SO WHERE **IS**... ?

ROWR!
Peirce

WHOEVER HEARD OF A DOG THAT KNITS **SWEATERS**? IT'S **RIDICULOUS**!
KLIK KLIK KLIK KLIK KLIK KLIK

DOGS ARE SUPPOSED TO FETCH STICKS! AND CATCH FRISBEES! AND...

...AND...

DON'T ASK.
Peirce

YOU'RE NEXT, NATE.
THANK YOU, CROWD! THANK YOU!

FOR MY REPORT, I WAS ASSIGNED THE TOPIC OF... PAUL REVERE!

HE WAS BORN IN HARVARD, NEBRASKA ON JANUARY 7TH, 1938. WHEN HE WAS 20 YEARS OLD, HE AND SOME FRIENDS STARTED A BAND.

AT FIRST, THEY CALLED THEMSELVES THE "DOWNBEATS," BUT EVENTUALLY THEY CHANGED THEIR NAME TO "PAUL REVERE AND THE RAIDERS."

ON STAGE, FOR NO APPARENT REASON, THEY WORE REVOLUTIONARY WAR COSTUMES! WEIRD, RIGHT?

ANYWAY, MY FAVORITE SONG OF THEIRS IS CALLED "KICKS"! AND IT GOES LIKE THIS:
AHEM!

THAT OLDIES STATION YOU LISTEN TO ALL THE TIME IS KILLING MY SOCIAL STUDIES GRADE.

YOU MAKE A SCRIBBLE, TEDDY, AND I'LL TURN IT INTO SOMETHING!
GOTCHA!
ZWIK
ZWIK

HA! THIS IS AN EASY ONE! IT ALREADY LOOKS JUST LIKE MY DAD!
WHAT? WHERE?

SEE THIS ROUND SHAPE RIGHT HERE?
THIS ONE?
NO, THIS BIG ONE.
THE HUGE ONE?

THAT'S HIS STOMACH!
OHHHH, YEAH!
SIGH...
Peirce

OKAY, WHAT'S THIS GAME CALLED?
THE SCRIBBLE GAME! I MAKE A SCRIBBLE, AND YOU TURN IT INTO SOMETHING!
ZWIK ZWIK

HOW DO I DO THAT?
BY ADDING LINES TO IT!

WHAT KIND OF LINES?
ANY KIND! WHATEVER KIND YOU WANT! NO LIMITS! GO CRAZY!

CAN THEY BE CURVY, OR...?
HE'S NOT VERY CREATIVE.
Peirce

I'M NOT VERY GOOD AT DRAWING.
DAD, RELAX! IT'S JUST A GAME!

THE SCRIBBLE GAME ISN'T ABOUT MAKING PERFECT DRAWINGS! IT'S ABOUT HAVING FUN! YOU CAN'T DO IT WRONG!

YES, YOU CAN.
IT'S A DUCK.
Peirce

NO OFFENSE, DAD, BUT TO PLAY THE SCRIBBLE GAME, YOU NEED A LITTLE IMAGINATION!

YOU WERE SUPPOSED TO TURN THE SCRIBBLE **INTO** SOMETHING!
I **DID!**

I TURNED IT INTO A FIGURE EIGHT!

IT ALREADY **WAS** A FIGURE EIGHT.
NO, IT WAS A SIX. SEE, I CLOSED THE LOOP.
Peirce

HERE, DAD.
HM? WHAT DO I DO WITH THIS?

DRAW SOMETHING! DRAW WHATEVER YOU WANT! THEN I'LL ANALYZE IT!

ANALYZING YOUR DOODLES WILL GIVE ME INSIGHTS INTO YOUR CREATIVITY... OR LACK THEREOF!

ON YOUR MARK... GET SET...
THE PRESSURE'S ON!
Peirce

I HATE TO BREAK THIS TO YOU, DAD, BUT YOUR DOODLES INDICATE A TOTAL LACK OF CREATIVITY.

FOR EXAMPLE, LOOK AT THE WAY YOU DREW THIS MAN RIGHT HERE...
THAT'S NOT A MAN, THAT'S A WOMAN.

YOUR DOODLES ALSO INDICATE YOU HAVEN'T DATED IN A WHILE.
Peirce

WHAT ARE YOU DOING?
BUILDING A SNOW PALACE!

WITH A GARBAGE CAN?
IT'S JUST LIKE MAKING A SAND CASTLE AT THE BEACH... ONLY BIGGER!
PAT PAT PAT

I'VE PACKED THIS CAN SOLID WITH SNOW!

NOW ALL I HAVE TO DO IS FLIP IT OVER, AND I'LL HAVE A PERFECTLY FORMED GIANT SNOW BRICK!

GRUNT!... A FEW DOZEN BRICKS... *OOF!* ...STACKED TOGETHER...

HMMPF!.. AND MY PALACE WILL BE COMPLETE!

YEEP!

CRUNCH!

A SNOW PALACE?
HE'S STARTING IN THE BASEMENT!
GET THE SHOVEL.
peirce

HOW ARE YOUR NEW YEAR'S RESO-LUTIONS GOING?
I DIDN'T MAKE ANY.
WHAT? WHY NOT?

BECAUSE THEY'RE **BOGUS**, THAT'S WHY NOT!
THEY'RE NOT BOGUS! THEY'RE AN OPPOR-TUNITY TO **IMPROVE** YOURSELF!

KLIK!
SHOOFF
PEIRCE

HOW COULD I POSSIBLY IMPROVE MYSELF?
BEATS ME.

SO YOU WANT ME TO MAKE A NEW YEAR'S RESOLUTION, FRANCIS? OKAY, FINE!

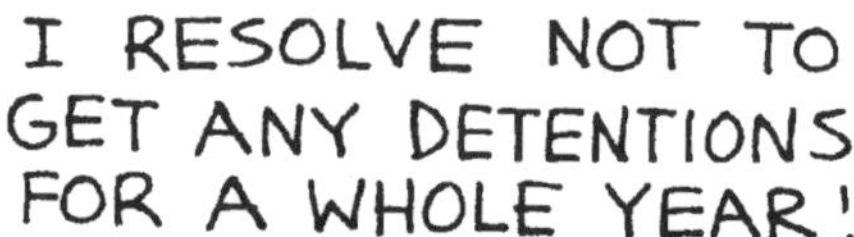
I RESOLVE NOT TO GET ANY DETENTIONS FOR A WHOLE YEAR!

MMPH!
HEH HEH!

WA HA HA HA HA HA HA
WHAT WE HAVE HERE IS A COMPLETE LACK OF RESPECT.
Peirce

WHAT ARE YOU CLOWNS CACKLING ABOUT?
NATE THINKS HE CAN GO A YEAR WITHOUT GETTING A DETENTION!

A YEAR? YOU COULDN'T GO A WEEK!
WHAT? I CAN GO A WEEK IN MY SLEEP, GINA!

OH, YEAH? THEN WHY DOES MRS. GODFREY GIVE YOU DETENTION EVERY DAY?
BECAUSE MRS. GODFREY IS A POWER-CRAZED GAS BAG!
Peirce

OOH, DID I SAY SOMETHING SHOCKING? EXCUSE ME FOR SPEAKING THE TRUTH!

I'LL BET YOU CAN'T GO A **WEEK** WITHOUT GETTING A DETENTION!
YOU'RE **ON**, GINA!

...AND IF I **WIN**, YOU HAVE TO PAY ME **TEN BUCKS**!
DONE!

...AND IF **I** WIN, **YOU** HAVE TO BE MY **PERSONAL SERVANT** FOR A **WHOLE DAY**!
WAIT, WHAT?

NO!... NO!
WE'RE SHAKING ON IT! **WE'RE SHAKING ON IT!!**
Peirce

YOU TWO ARE OUR WITNESSES! THE BET IS THAT NATE CAN'T GO A WEEK WITHOUT LANDING IN DETENTION!

...STARTING **NOW!**
NO, NOT STARTING NOW! STARTING **TOMORROW!**

WHAT? HOW COME?

BECAUSE HE HAS DETENTION **TODAY!**
HE GOT BUSTED FOR ASSAULTING THE SODA MACHINE!
IT ATE MY DOLLAR.
Peirce

IT'S A BET! IF YOU GET EVEN ONE DETENTION, YOU HAVE TO BE MY SERVANT FOR A DAY!
DON'T GET YOUR HOPES UP, GINA!

I'M GOING TO GET ZERO DETENTIONS, SO IT'LL BE TOUGH TOENAILS FOR YOU!
FUNNY YOU SHOULD MENTION TOENAILS!...

HOW ARE YOU AT GIVING PEDICURES?
!
!

IF I LOSE THIS BET, IT COULD HAVE A LASTING EFFECT ON MY MENTAL HEALTH.
Peirce

LET'S GO, LADIES!
WHOA, ELLEN! WHAT DO YOU THINK YOU'RE DOING?

DUH! SKATING, EINSTEIN!
UH, I DON'T THINK SO!

WE DIDN'T SPEND AN HOUR SHOVELING JUST SO YOU CAN HACK UP THE ICE WITH YOUR LITTLE FIGURE SKATES!

SO WHAT ARE WE SUPPOSED TO DO?
YOU'RE SUPPOSED TO PICK UP A SHOVEL! ...AND USE IT!

OOH! GIRLS! ARE YOU THINKING WHAT I'M THINKING?
THESE ARE THE PERFECT PROPS FOR OUR "LET IT SNOW" ROUTINE!

WHEEEEEEEE!
ARE YOU THINKING WHAT I'M THINKING?
GET THE PUCKS.
CHIP CHOP
CHIP CHIP CHOP
CHOP CHOP
CHIP CHIP
37

OKAY, OUR BET STARTS **NOW**! GOOD LUCK **NOT** GETTING DETENTION!
I DON'T **NEED** LUCK, GINA! THIS IS GOING TO BE **EASY**!

OH, **REALLY**? WHAT'S YOUR STRATEGY, GENIUS?
VERY SIMPLE! I'M GONNA DO WHAT **YOU** DO:

SHAMELESSLY SUCK UP TO THE TEACHERS!

WHA-?... SPUTTER!... **I** DON'T SHAMELESSLY SUCK UP TO...
MRS. GODFREY, YOU LOOK **FABULOUS**!
Peirce

YOU DON'T REALLY THINK SUCKING UP TO ALL THE TEACHERS WILL KEEP YOU OUT OF DETENTION, DO YOU?
WHY NOT?

SNORT! BECAUSE THEY'LL ALL KNOW YOU'RE A **FRAUD!** IT'LL NEVER WORK!
'SCUSE ME.

MRS. GODFREY, WOULD YOU LIKE SOME HELP ERASING THE BLACKBOARD?
WHY, **YES,** NATE! HOW **THOUGHTFUL!**

YEAH, YOU'RE RIGHT. IT'LL NEVER WORK.
Peirce

OH, NO! I FORGOT MY HOMEWORK!
HA! **NOW** YOU'LL GET DETENTION FOR **SURE**!

MR. GALVIN? I LEFT MY HOMEWORK ON MY KITCHEN TABLE. I APOLOGIZE, AND I PROMISE TO BRING IT TOMORROW.

THAT SOUNDS REASONABLE, NATE. I APPRECIATE YOUR HONESTY.

HE APPRECIATES MY HONESTY.
ARRGH!
peirce

THE WEEK'S HALF OVER, GINA, AND NATE HASN'T GOT A SINGLE DETENTION!
THERE'S STILL PLENTY OF TIME.

YEAH, BUT HE'S GOT ALL THE TEACHERS EATING OUT OF THE PALM OF HIS HAND!
OH, **PLEASE**! THE TEACHERS **HATE** HIM!
LITTERB
KEEP OUR

THE IDEA THAT HE COULD SUDDENLY BECOME THEIR **FAVORITE** IS A TOTAL **JOKE**!

...AND THEN THE CAMEL SAYS: "DUCK? **WHAT** DUCK?"
HA HA HA HA! VERY FUNNY, SIR!
!!
Peirce

I CAN'T BELIEVE THIS LITTLE ACT OF NATE'S IS WORKING!
WHAT DO YOU MEAN?

HE'S BASICALLY **BRIBING** ALL THE TEACHERS SO THEY WON'T GIVE HIM DETENTION!
BRIBING? OH, COME **ON**, GINA!

IT'S **TRUE!** AND I THINK PRINCIPAL NICHOLS SHOULD **KNOW** ABOUT IT!

BROWNIE?
OOH! DON'T MIND IF I DO!
Peirce

THIS IS **KILLING** YOU, ISN'T IT, GINA? I'VE GONE ALMOST A **WEEK** WITHOUT GETTING DETENTION!

ONLY ONE DAY TO GO! IF I MAKE IT THROUGH TOMORROW, I'LL WIN OUR LITTLE BET! IT'S **KILLING** YOU!

NATE, YOU'VE BEEN SO HELPFUL LATELY, I THOUGHT I'D GIVE YOU THE CHANCE TO CARRY THESE BOOKS TO MY CAR!

IT'S KILLING ME.
Peirce

OH, WHAT A MOVE!
HEY.

ULP! KIM!
I WANT YOU TO SKATE WITH ME.

ME? BUT...
I NEED TO PRACTICE MY LIFTS. LIKE THAT.

WHAT?? ARE YOU NUTS? I CAN'T DO THAT! YOU'RE TOO...

I MEAN... *KOFF!*... I... UH... I HURT MY ARM!... YEAH!... MY ARM!... SO I CAN'T...

SHUT UP.
! !

I HATE MYSELF.
Peirce

ONE DAY TO GO! IF I MAKE IT THROUGH TODAY WITHOUT GETTING A DETENTION, I WIN MY BET WITH GINA!
WR

YOU LOOK A LITTLE TENSE.
OBVI-OUSLY I'M TENSE, FRANCIS! IT'S **HARD WORK!**

DO YOU HAVE ANY IDEA WHAT IT'S LIKE TO SUCK UP TO OUR TEACHERS ALL THE... OH... HEH HEH...
HA HA

REMEMBER WHO YOU'RE TALKING TO!
YEAH, WHAT AM I **SAYING**? THAT'S YOUR **LIFE!**
HA HA HA
HA HA

NATE, I'VE BEEN **DELIGHTED** WITH YOUR BEHAVIOR THESE PAST FEW DAYS!
OH... UH... YEAH... THANKS.

I'M HOPING THIS IS THE START OF A **NEW** NATE WRIGHT, WHO BEHAVES THIS WAY **ALL THE TIME**!

I'M PARA-LYZED.
HELLO?
SNAP SNAP
Peirce

GETTING **NERVOUS**, GINA? IF NATE DOESN'T GET A DETENTION BETWEEN NOW AND 3:00, HE WINS YOUR BET!

I'LL ADMIT, I'M SURPRISED HE HASN'T SCREWED UP YET. BUT HE WILL.

WATER ALWAYS SEEKS ITS OWN LEVEL.

MEANWHILE...
?
CLUNK! CLUNK!
Peirce

IS THERE A PROBLEM, NATE?
THE WATER FOUNTAIN IS BUSTED.
CLUNK CLUNK

THAT'S ODD, IT WAS WORKING THIS MORNING. LET ME TAKE A LOOK.

HMMM...
HEY, THERE'S SOMETHING STUCK IN THERE!
POP!

FOOSH!

SPLUTTER! I'M DRENCHED!!
SORRY SORRY SORRY SORRY SORRY

NATE, WHAT ON EARTH...
I... IT... I DIDN'T...
AH-HA!

I KNEW IT! I KNEW YOU'D SCREW UP! I WIN THE BET, 'CAUSE YOU'RE ABOUT TO GET DETENTION!
Peirce

WHAT BET? AND WHO SAYS HE'S ABOUT TO GET DETENTION?
! ! !

WHAT'S ALL THIS ABOUT A **BET**, YOU TWO?
UH... IT... HEH HEH...

I BET NATE THAT HE COULDN'T GO A **WEEK** WITHOUT GETTING DETENTION!
... AND I'M ALMOST THERE! ONLY THREE HOURS TO GO!

I SEE. WELL, NATE, THAT CERTAINLY EXPLAINS YOUR RECENT BEHAVIOR...
peirce

... BUT, GINA, IT DOESN'T EXPLAIN **YOURS**.
?!
!

FRANCIS, DID YOU SEE "HOARDERS" THE OTHER NIGHT?
WHAT'S THAT?

IT'S A SHOW ABOUT PEOPLE WHO HOARD STUFF.
SCHOOL ZONE
WHAT KIND OF STUFF?

ANYTHING! MAGAZINES, CLOTHES, FOOD... ALL KINDS OF JUNK!
IF IT'S JUNK, WHY DON'T THEY THROW IT AWAY?

BECAUSE TO THEM, IT'S NOT JUNK! TO THEM, IT'S VALUABLE!

IT'S PRETTY INTERESTING. YOU SHOULD WATCH IT.

I DON'T NEED TO WATCH IT.
WHAT EXACTLY DO YOU MEAN BY "CLEAN UP"?
Peirce

SO YOU BET THAT NATE WOULD GET DETENTION?
WELL, IT... *GULP!*... IT WASN'T REALLY A BET...

IT WAS LIKE... I WAS GIVING HIM INCENTIVE NOT TO GET DETENTION! I WAS TRYING TO MOTI-VATE HIM!
I SEE.

THEN WHY WERE YOU SO DELIGHTED A MOMENT AGO WHEN YOU THOUGHT I WAS ABOUT TO PUNISH HIM?
I... UM...

BECAUSE SHE'S EVIL.
I'LL HANDLE THIS, NATE.
Peirce

YOU'RE FAMILIAR WITH THE SCHOOL HANDBOOK, GINA, SO YOU SHOULD KNOW THAT BETTING IS PROHIBITED AT P.S. 38.

I'M DISAPPOINTED IN YOU.
BUT... IT WASN'T JUST **ME**! AREN'T YOU DISAPPOINTED IN **NATE**, TOO?

NO... WITH NATE, IT'S NOT DISAPPOINTMENT.

IT'S MORE LIKE NUMB ACCEPTANCE.
HA! TAKE **THAT**, GINA!
Peirce

MRS. GODFREY, WAIT! AREN'T YOU GOING TO SEND NATE TO DETENTION?
NO, I'M NOT, GINA.

B-BUT... HE SPRAYED WATER ON YOU!
...WHICH WAS OBVIOUSLY AN ACCIDENT!

NATE WAS CLEARLY JUST AS SURPRISED AS I WAS!
OH, YEAH! I WAS SHOCKED! STUNNED!

FLABBERGASTED! HORNSWOGGLED! GOBSMACKED!
WHY DON'T WE ALL GO TO OUR NEXT CLASS?
Peirce

THE DAY'S ALMOST OVER, NATE! ANY DETENTIONS YET?
IT DOESN'T MATTER ANYMORE, FRANCIS!

MRS. GODFREY JUST DECLARED OUR BET NULL AND VOID! SO EVEN IF I DO GET DETENTION, I DON'T HAVE TO BE GINA'S PERSONAL SERVANT!

NOT ONLY THAT, MRS. GODFREY ACTUALLY TOLD GINA SHE WAS DISAPPOINTED IN HER!

WOW!
SHUT UP.
THIS IS THE HAPPIEST DAY OF MY LIFE!
Peirce

RRRRINNGG!
THERE'S THE BELL! END OF THE DAY!

...AND **WHAT** A DAY! WHAT AN AMAZING DAY!

DON'T YOU AGREE, GINA? DON'T YOU THINK IT'S BEEN AN AMAZING DAY?

I HATE YOU.
HEAR THAT, GANG? IT KEEPS GETTING BETTER!
Peirce

HI, NATE! HOW WAS SCHOOL?
IT... WAS... AWESOME!

I SPRAYED WATER ALL OVER MRS. GOD-FREY, AND I DIDN'T EVEN GET IN TROUBLE FOR IT!

INSTEAD, GUESS WHO GOT CHEWED OUT? GINA!! LITTLE MISS PERFECT!

I MEANT "HOW WAS SCHOOL" IN THE TESTS-QUIZZES-HOMEWORK SENSE.
OH, COME ON, DAD. ONLY TEACHERS CARE ABOUT THAT STUFF!
Peirce

SPITSY! COME HERE!

SEE THAT, SPITSY? THAT'S A CAT!

CAT BAD! CAT ENEMY! GOT IT?

OKAY, THEN... YOU'RE OUT FOR A WALK, AND SUDDENLY YOU SEE A CAT! WHAT DO YOU DO?

WURF!

WURRRRRRF...

! !
CRUMBLE!

WHIMPER!

OWOOOOOO
I CAN'T TAKE IT.

PRINCIPAL NICHOLS, CAN WE HAVE A PEP RALLY BEFORE OUR BIG GAME AGAINST PRESSWICK?

WE CAN TOSS SOME CONFETTI AROUND, SING THE SCHOOL FIGHT SONG...
P.S. 38 DOESN'T HAVE A FIGHT SONG.

WE DON'T?
NO.

...NOT YET!
UH-OH.
Peirce

SO, NATE, I TAKE IT YOU'RE GOING TO WRITE A SCHOOL FIGHT SONG?
YOU **BET** I AM!

WELL, PLEASE MAKE SURE YOU GO ABOUT IT IN A POSITIVE, CONSTRUCTIVE WAY.

I DON'T WANT A REPEAT OF THE TIME YOU PROPOSED A SCHOOL MOTTO.
WHAT WAS WRONG WITH MY MOTTO?

"SUCKING THE LIFE OUT OF STUDENTS FOR ALMOST A CENTURY" ISN'T WHAT WE'RE LOOKING FOR, SON.
YEAH, I SEE YOUR POINT. TOO WORDY.
Peirce

HERE'S THE SCOOP, GUYS: DID YOU KNOW THAT P.S. 38 DOESN'T HAVE A FIGHT SONG?
F

I ASKED PRINCIPAL NICHOLS WHY, AND HE SAID NOBODY EVER **WROTE** ONE!

...UNTIL **NOW**, THAT IS!
F

GENTLEMEN... **I AM THAT NOBODY!**
I'VE ALWAYS SAID THAT ABOUT YOU!
Peirce

I'M STUDYING A BUNCH OF FAMOUS FIGHT SONGS TO GET SOME IDEAS FOR MY OWN!

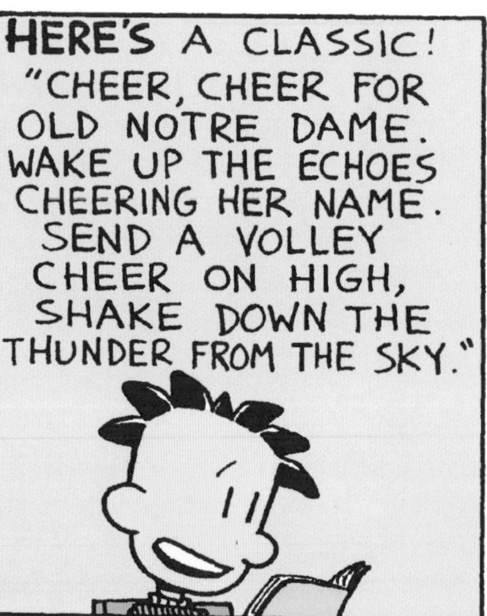
HERE'S A CLASSIC! "CHEER, CHEER FOR OLD NOTRE DAME. WAKE UP THE ECHOES CHEERING HER NAME. SEND A VOLLEY CHEER ON HIGH, SHAKE DOWN THE THUNDER FROM THE SKY."

"WAKE UP THE ECHOES." THAT'S COOL.
YEAH. EXCEPT IT DOESN'T REALLY MAKE SENSE FOR P.S. 38.

THE ONLY ECHOES AROUND HERE ARE IN THE THIRD-FLOOR BATHROOM.
MIGHT BE TOUGH TO WORK THAT INTO A SONG LYRIC.
Peirce

IT'S **SHOCKING** THAT P.S. 38 DOESN'T HAVE A FIGHT SONG! IT'S COMPLETELY UNACCEPTABLE!

HAVING NO FIGHT SONG TELLS EVERYBODY WE'RE A **SECOND-CLASS INSTITUTION**!

I THOUGHT WE WERE A SECOND-CLASS INSTITUTION BECAUSE THE **FRENCH FRIES** IN THE CAFETORIUM ARE ALWAYS **UNDERCOOKED**!

SOGGY FRIES ARE AN **OUTRAGE**!
CHAD, LET'S TRY TO STAY ON TOPIC.
Peirce

GUYS! HOW DO YOU LIKE MY FIGHT SONG SO FAR?

"GIVE A CHEER FOR P.S. 38! BOBCATS! BOBCATS! WE ARE REALLY GREAT!"

"WHEN YOU PLAY US, LOSING IS YOUR FATE. AND BY THE WAY, THIS SONG WAS WRITTEN BY NATE!"

MOST SONGWRITERS DON'T INCLUDE THEIR OWN NAMES IN THEIR LYRICS.
I'M NOT LIKE MOST SONGWRITERS.
NO KIDDING.
Peirce

VALENTINES

HMMPH!

NOPE.

LAME.

YECCH.

CAN I HELP YOU FIND SOMETHING, YOUNG MAN?
YEAH...

DO YOU HAVE ANY THAT SAY, "WHENEVER YOU DECIDE TO DUMP THAT LOSER YOU'RE GOING OUT WITH, I'LL BE AROUND"?

"A CARD FOR EVERY OCCASION." HA!
THERE'S ONLY ONE O IN "LOSER."
Peirce

NATE! HOW'S THE FIGHT SONG GOING?
EXCUSE, PLEASE. WHAT "FIGHT SONG" IS?

IT'S A SONG YOU PLAY TO GET EVERY-BODY PSYCHED UP, ARTUR. AT SPORTING EVENTS AND STUFF.
OH HO! YES, IN BELARUS WE HAVE SUCH SONGS!

HERE ONE IS CALLED "BALLAD OF THE UNCOMFORTABLE GOATHERD."

AS I WATCH MY GOATS FROLIC IN THE MEADOW... I NOTICE A PAINFUL GAS BUBBLE IN MY LOWER ABDOMEN...
STOP.
Peirce

I THINK MOST FIGHT SONGS ARE LAME! THEY'RE ALL "WE'RE SO GREAT, WE LOVE OUR SCHOOL," BLAH BLAH BLAH!

...BUT SHOULDN'T A FIGHT SONG HAVE SOME **FIGHTING** IN IT? **MY** SONG WILL HAVE OUR OPPONENTS SHAKING IN THEIR BOOTS!

"WE ARE THE BOBCATS, HEAR US ROAR. FLESH-EATING BOBCATS, KNEE-DEEP IN GORE."

"WE ARE BLOODTHIRSTY, VICIOUS AND MEAN. WE'LL BITE OFF YOUR HEAD AND RIP OUT YOUR SPLEEN."
CATCHY!
WHAT'S A SPLEEN?
peirce

NOW THAT I'VE WRITTEN THE LYRICS TO OUR NEW FIGHT SONG, ALL WE NEED TO DO IS SET 'EM TO MUSIC!

LET'S HAVE AN "ENSLAVE THE MOLLUSK" JAM SESSION AFTER SCHOOL, FRANCIS!
BUT WE'RE A **ROCK** BAND!

FIGHT SONGS ARE USUALLY PLAYED BY **MARCHING** BANDS!
HM. GOOD POINT.

CHAD. MY HOUSE. 3:30. BRING YOUR OBOE.
ROGER!

RATS! WE **STILL** SOUND LOUSY!

WITH ONLY FIVE OF US, IT'S TOUGH TO GET THAT BIG "FIGHT SONG" SOUND.
YOU'RE RIGHT, TEDDY.
WELL, ISN'T THE ANSWER SIMPLE?

WE JUST NEED MORE INSTRU-
SSH! NO!

DID SOMEONE SAY "MORE INSTRUMENTS"?
BAD MOVE, FRANCIS.

PRINCIPAL NICHOLS, I'VE BEEN WORKING ON A FIGHT SONG, AND...
AH... YES, ABOUT THAT, NATE...

MRS. SHIPULSKI HEARD ME MENTION IT, AND SHE DECIDED SHE'D TRY HER HAND AT WRITING A FIGHT SONG!
SHE DID?

SHE CAME UP WITH A HOT LITTLE TUNE CALLED "BOBCAT PRIDE"!
SHE DID?

SHE DID?
I'VE HAD EIGHT MILLION HITS ON YOUTUBE!

NUTS. I PUT ALL THAT TIME INTO WRITING A SCHOOL FIGHT SONG, AND MRS. SHIPULSKI BEAT ME TO IT!

YEAH, I HEARD! "BOBCAT PRIDE"!
MAYBE THERE'S STILL HOPE FOR **MY** SONG!

MAYBE **HERS** WON'T CATCH ON!
HEY, GUYS! LISTEN TO MY NEW RING-TONE!

♫ BOBCAT PRIDE... ♫
BOBCAT SPIRIT...
FAR AND WIDE...
CAN'T YOU HEAR IT...
ET TU, CHAD?
Peirce

WHAT THE...?
WAIT HERE, SPITSY.
SPITSY

FRANCIS, WHAT ARE YOU **DOING**?
I'M WALKING PICKLES!

YOU'RE WALKING YOUR **CAT**? **NOBODY** WALKS **CATS**, FRANCIS!
WHY NOT?

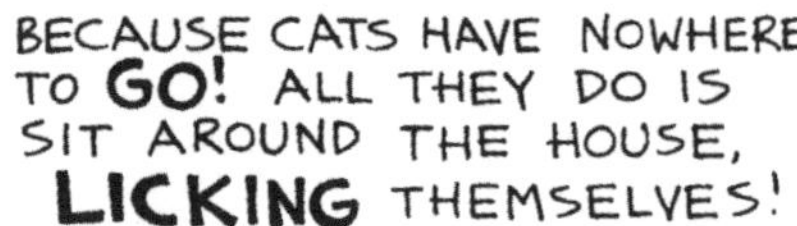
BECAUSE CATS HAVE NOWHERE TO **GO**! ALL THEY DO IS SIT AROUND THE HOUSE, **LICKING** THEMSELVES!

THEY'RE NOT LIKE **DOGS**! DOGS GO TO THE PARK, TO THE LAKE, TO THE WOODS...
PICKLES HAS SOMEWHERE TO GO. SHE HAS A PLAY DATE WITH A FRIEND.

A **PLAY DATE**?
THEY ALWAYS HAVE FUN TOGETHER!

DOING **WHAT**, COUGHING UP **HAIRBALLS**?
WURF!

USUALLY, THEY JUST WRESTLE!
WURF!
HEE HEE!
MYOWR!
FSST!
TEE HEE!
WURF!
ROWR!
HEE!
RUFF!
Peirce

WOW! TEDDY! CHECK OUT THAT ICICLE!
IT'S HUGE!

LET'S TRY TO SNAP IT OFF!
CAREFUL! DON'T BUST IT!

KRRK!
YES!

OOF! THIS THING'S HEAVY!
WHAT ARE WE SUPPOSED TO DO WITH IT?

IT'S NOT LIKE WE CAN REALLY PLAY WITH IT.
LET'S SMASH IT AGAINST THAT TREE!

CRUNCH!
YAAAH!

HA HA HA
HA HA HA
HA HA HA

HEH HEH...
HA... HEH...

THE AWESOMENESS DIDN'T LAST AS LONG AS I THOUGHT IT WOULD.
WHAT ELSE CAN WE BREAK?
Peirce

CLASS, YOUR SIXTH GRADE BOOK BUDDIES ARE HERE!
HI, MRS. BIGBEE!

HELLO, NATE.
HEY, WHERE'S MY BOOK BUDDY?

I'M AFRAID PETER'S ABSENT TODAY... BUT THERE'S **ANOTHER** CHILD WHO NEEDS A BUDDY.
MIRANDA? WILL YOU COME HERE, PLEASE?

NO!
SHE MAY HAVE HAD A BIT TOO MUCH SUGAR AT SNACK TIME.

NATE, I'M GOING TO PAIR YOU WITH MIRANDA!
OKAY.

SHE CAN BE A BIT... ER... CHALLENGING, BUT SHE'S A VERY BRIGHT YOUNG LADY!

JUST BE POSITIVE AND ENCOURAGING, AND I'M SURE SHE'LL RESPOND VERY WELL!
POSITIVE. ENCOURAGING. GOTCHA.

WELL, **HI** THERE, MIRAN-
YOU HAVE STUPID HAIR.

I KNOW YOU, MIRANDA! DO YOU REMEMBER ME?
NO.

LAST FALL! I WAS HELPING OUT ON SCHOOL PICTURE DAY! REMEMBER?
NO.

DO YOU REMEMBER WEARING A PINKISH-PURPLISH DRESS?
NO.

DO YOU REMEMBER BITING ME?
HA HA! YEEEEAH!
Peirce

OKAY, MIRANDA, I'M YOUR SUBSTITUTE BOOK BUDDY! WHAT DO YOU WANT TO READ?

I WANT TO READ THE LABEL ON THE BOTTOM OF YOUR SNEAKERS.

WHILE YOU'RE LYING ON YOUR BACK.
AFTER I **DECK** YOU.

I'M SCARED OF MY BOOK BUDDY.
SHE WATCHES A LOT OF MMA.
Peirce

"AND THEN THE LITTLE DUCK SWAM UNDER THE BR... THE BRI... BRUH..."
AH! A **TEACHABLE MOMENT**, AS WE SAY IN THE BOOK BUDDY BIZ!

MIRANDA, WHAT DO WE DO WHEN WE COME TO A WORD WE CAN'T READ?

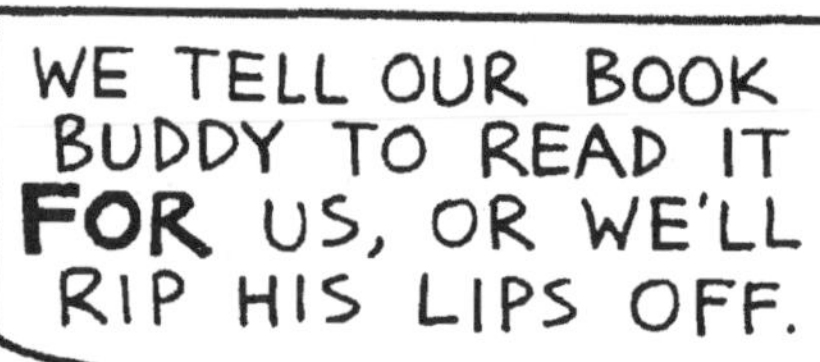
WE TELL OUR BOOK BUDDY TO READ IT **FOR** US, OR WE'LL RIP HIS LIPS OFF.

"BRIDGE."
"BRIDGE."
AWW! SO **SWEET**!
Peirce

THIS BOOK STINKS. I WANT TO READ A DIFFERENT BOOK.

I WANT TO READ A BOOK ABOUT BIG KIDS TRYING TO BOSS LITTLE KIDS AROUND, BUT THE LITTLE KIDS ARE LIKE: I DON'T THINK SO!

...AND THEN ALL THE BIG KIDS GET EATEN BY DINOSAURS, AND THE LITTLE KIDS TAKE OVER THE WORLD. THE END.

I WANT TO READ A BOOK LIKE THAT RIGHT NOW!
I'M ON IT.
Peirce

I HATE BOOK BUDDY TIME.
NOW, NOW, MIRANDA!

WE'LL NEVER FIND OUT WHAT HAPPENS TO BIPPITY BUNNY WITH **THAT** ATTITUDE! KEEP READING!
SIGH...

"BIPPITY WAVED GOODBYE TO GRANNY GRUMBLE AND STARTED ON HIS WAY. SOON HE MET A... A..."
"PEDDLER"

A PEDAL IS PART OF A BICYCLE! SO BIPPITY MUST HAVE MET SOME-ONE RIDING A **BIKE**!
BUT...

THAT'S NOT WHAT IT MEANS!

IF SOMEONE WAS RIDING A **BIKE**, IT WOULD BE SPELLED P·E·D·A·L·E·R! A **PEDDLER** IS SOMEBODY WHO **SELLS** STUFF!

YOU'RE EVEN STUPIDER THAN YOU LOOK.

WHEN I WAS IN FIRST GRADE, WE WERE **AFRAID** OF SIXTH-GRADERS.
I **LIKE** BOOK BUDDY TIME!
Peirce

CLASS, WE HAVE A **SPECIAL GUEST** WITH US TODAY!

METEOROLOGIST CHIP CAVENDISH FROM CHANNEL 12 IS HERE TO TELL US ABOUT...
HOLD IT! **HOLD IT!**

YOU'RE THE GUY WHO STOLE WINK SUMMERS' JOB!

UH...
CRIPES.
DON'T LISTEN TO HIM, GANG! HE'S A **FRAUD!**
peirce

NATE, TAKE YOUR SEAT AND PAY ATTENTION TO MR. CAVENDISH.
I DON'T **WANT** TO PAY ATTENTION TO HIM!

I WANT TO HEAR ABOUT THE WEATHER FROM **WINK SUMMERS!** BUT THE GENIUSES AT CHANNEL 12 CANNED WINK AND BROUGHT IN **THIS** GUY!

THEY DIDN'T CARE ABOUT WINK! THEY ONLY CARED ABOUT GIVING THEIR VIEWERS SOME **EYE CANDY!**

HE BROUGHT **CANDY?**
IT'S AN EXPRESSION, CHAD. RELAX.
Peirce

HI, KIDS! I'M CHIP CAVENDISH, CHIEF METEOROLOGIST FOR CHANNEL 12 ACTION NEWS!

I'M HERE TO TALK TO YOU ABOUT WEATHER! I'LL TELL YOU WHAT CAUSES WIND, RAIN, SNOW, AND SO ON!

...AND IF YOU DON'T UNDERSTAND SOMETHING I'VE SAID, JUST RAISE YOUR HAND AND ASK!

HOW DO YOU SLEEP AT NIGHT, KNOWING YOU'VE DESTROYED WINK SUMMERS' LIFE?
TELL YOU WHAT, LET'S SAVE THE QUESTIONS 'TIL THE END.
Peirce

THAT WAS FASCINATING! LET'S HEAR IT FOR CHIP CAVENDISH FROM CHANNEL 12, EVERYONE!
CLAP
CLAP
CLAP
CLAP
CLAP

CAN I HAVE YOUR AUTOGRAPH?
WHY, SURE, YOUNG MAN!

UH... WHAT'S ALL THIS WRITING ON HERE?
NOTHING, NOTHING. JUST SIGN IT.

"I, CHIP CAVENDISH, DO HEREBY RESIGN AS CHANNEL 12's CHIEF METEOR-OLOGIST..."
WHA-? HOW DID THAT GET THERE?
Peirce

WHAT A FIASCO! I CAN'T BELIEVE WE HAD TO SIT THERE AND LISTEN TO **CHIP CAVENDISH** TALK ABOUT THE WEATHER!

WHAT DOES **HE** KNOW ABOUT THE WEATHER, ANYWAY? COMPARED TO WINK SUMMERS, THAT GUY'S A TOTAL **AMATEUR**!

"CHIP CAVENDISH"! *SNORT!* WHAT A PHONY! I'LL BET THAT'S NOT EVEN HIS **REAL NAME**!

HAVE YOU CONSIDERED THE POSSIBILITY THAT "WINK SUMMERS" ISN'T A REA
NO.
Peirce

HOW COME YOU'RE ALWAYS TALKING ABOUT THIS WINK SUMMERS DUDE?
BECAUSE HE'S MY FAVORITE TV WEATHER GUY!

OKAY, BUT HOW DO YOU KNOW HE WAS SO DEVASTATED ABOUT LOSING HIS JOB TO CHIP CAVENDISH?
FROM HIS BLOG.
KLIK!

CHIPCAVENDISH RUINEDMYCAREER. BLOGSPOT.COM

AH.
WANT ME TO ADD YOU TO HIS EMAIL LIST?

ARRGH! IT JUST DOESN'T **ADD UP!**

CAN I HELP, DAD?
NOT UNLESS YOU CAN BALANCE MY CHECKBOOK.

I CAN'T DO **THAT**, BUT I CAN **DE-STRESS** YOU WITH THIS EMPTY PLASTIC BOTTLE!

SEE WHAT I MEAN?
THUNK THUNK THUNK THUNK
SAY, THAT **DOES** FEEL GOOD!

THUNK THUNK **THUNKA** THUNK THUNK THUNK **THUNKA** THUNK

THUNKA **THUNK** THUNK THUNKA **THUNK** THUNK **THUNKITY THONK**

CHUCKA **POW** CHUCKA **POW** CHUCKA CHUCK **POW** P-P-**POW!**...

ENOUGH!
Peirce

THUNK THUNK THUNK THUNK THUNK THUNK THUNK THUNK

AH, **HERE'S** WHAT I LIKE TO SEE! A YOUNG MAN DOING HIS HOMEWORK!
HOMEWORK?

THIS ISN'T HOMEWORK! I'M WRITING A **PETITION**!
A PETITION TO DO WHAT?

TO RESTORE WINK SUMMERS TO HIS RIGHTFUL PLACE AS CHANNEL 12'S CHIEF METEOROLOGIST! TO UNDO A MAJOR **INJUSTICE**!

SO THIS IS **BIGGER** THAN HOMEWORK.
RIGHT. TEN THOUSAND SIGNATURES, **MINIMUM**.
Peirce

HI, MISTER, WILL YOU SIGN THIS PETITION TO HELP WINK SUMMERS GET HIS JOB BACK?
AH! THE **WEATHERMAN!**

I WANTED TO BE A WEATHERMAN. I USED TO SPEND **HOURS** STUDYING CHARTS AND MAPS.

TRAGICALLY, THOUGH, MY DREAMS WERE DASHED. MY PARENTS THOUGHT METEOROLOGY WAS A FRIVOLOUS PURSUIT.

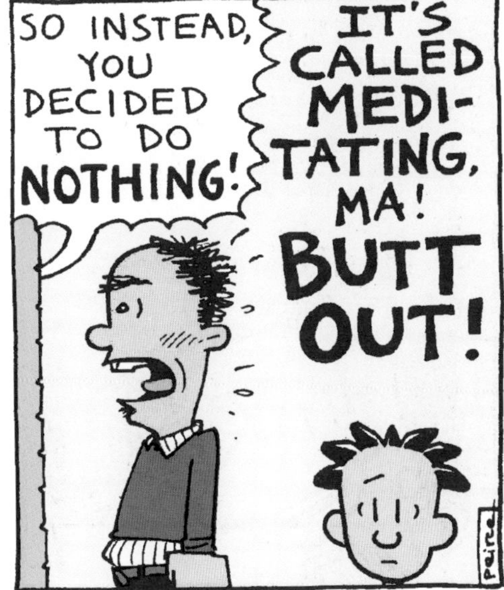
SO INSTEAD, YOU DECIDED TO DO **NOTHING!**
IT'S CALLED MEDITATING, MA! BUTT OUT!
peirce

HI, LADY. WILL YOU SIGN MY PETITION TO GET WINK SUMMERS REINSTATED AS CHANNEL 12'S CHIEF METEOR-OLOGIST ?
WINK SUMMERS?

WINK SUMMERS SAID MY WEDDING DAY WOULD BE WARM AND SUNNY!

DO YOU KNOW WHAT IT DID? IT HAILED!

MY AUNT PATTY GOT A CONCUSSION!
YOU'RE NOT GOING TO SIGN MY PETITION, ARE YOU?
Peirce

HI, MISTER, WOULD YOU LIKE TO...?
OOH! ARE YOU SELLING COOKIES?

UH... NO, I'M COLLECTING SIGNATURES TO GET WINK SUMMERS HIS JOB BACK AS CHANNEL 12'S CHIEF METEOR-OLOGIST.
NO COOKIES?

NO CANDY BARS? NO GOURMET POP-CORN? NO FRUIT BASKETS?
TELL YOU WHAT...

SIGN THIS AND I'LL GIVE YOU HALF A ROLL OF MENTOS.
DONE!
Peirce

...AND I'M HOPING IF ENOUGH PEOPLE SIGN THIS PETITION, CHANNEL 12 WILL GIVE WINK SUMMERS HIS JOB BACK!

BUT THEN WHAT WILL HAPPEN TO THE YOUNG FELLOW WHO **REPLACED** HIM?
CHIP CAVENDISH? WHO **CARES**?

HE'S NOT THERE BECAUSE HE'S A GOOD METEOROLOGIST! HE'S THERE BECAUSE HE LOOKS LIKE A **J. CREW MODEL**!

EXACTLY.
ROWR!
MRS. O'MALLEY! **HELLO**? **FOCUS**!
SNAP!
SNAP!
Peirce

WELCOME TO CHANNEL 12! HOW MAY I HELP YOU?
CAN YOU GIVE THIS TO THE STATION MANAGER?

IT'S A PETITION TO GET WINK SUMMERS HIS JOB BACK AS CHIEF METEOROLOGIST!

MY GOODNESS, WHAT A LOT OF SIGNATURES!
YUP! FIVE HUNDRED PEOPLE!

...480 OF WHOM HAVE IDENTICAL HAND-WRITING.
IT'S A VERY CLOSE NEIGH-BORHOOD.
peirce

THERE GO JENNY AND ARTUR.
DON'T START.

DON'T START WHAT?
DON'T START WHINING!

"POOR ME! WHY, OH WHY DOES JENNY LIKE ARTUR IN-STEAD OF ME?"

I'M NOT GOING TO START WHINING, FRANCIS! I DON'T WHINE!

AND BY THE WAY, I HAPPEN TO KNOW WHY JENNY PREFERS ARTUR TO ME!
YOU DO?

YEAH! BECAUSE HE'S NICE! HE'S WAY NICER THAN I AM!

I MEAN, I'M NOT A JERK OR ANYTHING... BUT SOME-TIMES I DO JERKY THINGS.
LIKE WHAT?

FIVE SECONDS LATER...
OH.
SEE, ARTUR WOULD NEVER DO THAT!
Peirce

WHAT'S WRONG, TEDDY?
THERE MIGHT BE NO BASE-BALL THIS YEAR.

IF WE CAN'T FIND A SPONSOR, WE CAN'T HAVE A TEAM.
WHAT ABOUT OUR SPON-SOR FROM LAST SEASON? McSWEEN'S MONEY MANAGEMENT?

MR. McSWEEN CAN'T DO IT THIS YEAR.
WHY **NOT**?

HE'S IN JAIL.
YEAH, BUT DOES A LITTLE PONZI SCHEME MEAN HE CAN'T SPRING FOR **UNIFORMS**?
Peirce

HERE'S THE DEAL, GUYS. IF WE DON'T GET A BUSINESS TO SPONSOR US, OUR BASEBALL TEAM GOES DOWN THE TUBES!

WE NEED TO FIND A SPONSOR, **FAST**.
WANT ME TO TALK TO MY GRAM?

WHAT DOES SHE DO?
SHE PLAYS BRIDGE, AND SHE KNITS HATS FOR NEWBORN BABIES!

I DON'T THINK THAT'LL FIT ON A BASEBALL JERSEY, CHAD.
AND SHE BAKES **KILLER** DOUBLE-CHOCOLATE BROWNIES!
Peirce

GORDIE, MY MAN!
HI, NATE! WHAT'S GOIN' ON?

I'LL GET RIGHT TO IT: DOES KLASSIC KOMIX WANT TO SPONSOR MY LITTLE LEAGUE TEAM?
HMM... WE'LL HAVE TO ASK WAYNE.

HE'S THE ONE WHO'LL BE ABLE TO GIVE YOU AN ANSWER!

OH, GOODY.
MUMBLE MUMBLE MUMBLE MUMBLE MUMBLE MUMBLE MUMBLE MUMBLE
Peirce

UH... WAYNE, I WAS WONDERING IF KLASSIC KOMIX CAN SPONSOR MY BASEBALL TEAM.

GRRRRRRRRRRR...

MUMBLE MUMBLE MUMB
LE MUMBLE MUMBLE MUMB
MBLE MUMBLE MUMBLE

I'M PRETTY SURE THAT WAS A "NO."
SORRY, DUDE.

SORRY WAYNE WON'T SPONSOR YOUR BASE-BALL TEAM, NATE.
HMPH.

I TRIED TO CHANGE HIS MIND, BUT... WELL, WHO KNOWS WHAT HIS REASONS ARE...

HEE HEE HE HEE HEE HEE HEE HEE HE HEE HEE HE

MAYBE HE'S JUST NOT A "SPORTS" KIND OF GUY.
YOU THINK?

HEADING HOME, NATE?
NO, GORDIE, THERE'S WORK TO BE DONE.

MY BASEBALL TEAM NEEDS A SPONSOR, AND I WON'T REST UNTIL I FIND ONE!

I'LL VISIT EVERY STORE IN THIS MALL IF I HAVE TO!

...STARTING WITH VICTORIA'S SECRET.
ROWR!
GOOD THINK-ING.

HOW ABOUT HERE?
PERFECT!

NOT ANOTHER SOUL AS FAR AS THE EYE CAN SEE!
WE'RE TOTALLY ISOLATED!

THAT'S WHY I LIKE IT!
GIGGLE! OH, TODD!

TONG!
!

GROANN..
TODD! HONEY! ARE YOU...?

HI.

AH! JACKPOT!

FOUND IT, DAD!

I'M TERRIBLY SORRY.
WE'RE NEAR A GOLF COURSE?
NOT REALLY.

DID YOU GUYS HAVE ANY LUCK FINDING A SPONSOR?
NOPE. WHAT ABOUT YOU?

NOTHIN'. AND I TRIED EVERY STORE AND KIOSK IN THE MALL.
WAIT, YOU ASKED **KIOSKS** TO SPONSOR US?

SURE, WHY NOT?
IT'S JUST... HAVING A KIOSK AS A SPONSOR SOUNDS KIND OF LAME.

IT'S LIKE BEING SPONSORED BY A VENDING MACHINE.
WHENEVER I HEAR THE WORD "KIOSK," I THINK OF WAL-RUSES!
PEIRCE

THEIR HAND-CUT CRULLERS ARE THE BEST IN TOWN, THEIR CINNAMON ROLLS ARE TOP-NOTCH, AND THEIR ECLAIRS ARE **INCREDIBLE**!

NOW THAT WE'VE FOUND A SPONSOR, I CAN PUT TOGETHER A PRACTICE SCHEDULE!
THINK WE'LL BE GOOD THIS YEAR, COACH?
OACH

I DON'T SEE WHY NOT! OUR ROSTER LOOKS PRETTY STRONG!

NATE WRIGHT, TEDDY ORTIZ, FRANCIS POPE, TIM CRESSLY...
THAT'S **KIM** CRESSLY.

GAH!
C'MERE, PUNKIN'.

K-KIM! **YOU'RE** ON OUR BASEBALL TEAM?
OBVIOUSLY.

MY FAMILY'S BUSINESS IS SPONSORING THE TEAM.

CRESSLY'S BAKERY? THAT'S **YOU**?
WELL, **DUH**. HOW MANY CRESSLYS DO YOU THINK THERE **ARE**?
! !

AT THE MOMENT, ONE TOO MANY.
YOU'RE CUTE WHEN YOU ACT STUPID.
PEIRCE

WAIT A MINUTE, KIM! HOW COME YOU'RE PLAYING BASEBALL? GIRLS PLAY SOFTBALL!
THERE IS NO SOFTBALL.

NOT ENOUGH GIRLS SIGNED UP, SO THE LEAGUE DISBANDED AND I SWITCHED TO BASEBALL.

SO NOW WE'RE TEAMMATES.
YEAH, THAT'S... THAT'S...

INCREDIBLY ROMANTIC.
NO!
Peirce

PLAYING ON THE SAME TEAM WILL BE THE MOST TIME WE'VE SPENT TOGETHER SINCE WE BROKE UP.
WHA-? **HOLD** IT!

WE NEVER "BROKE UP," KIM, BECAUSE WE WERE NEVER GOING OUT IN THE **FIRST** PLACE! WAKE UP TO **REALITY**!

SO WHAT I JUST HEARD YOU SAY WAS: WE NEVER BROKE UP.

CRIPES.
OUR LOVE IS A RED-HOT FLAME THAT CAN NEVER BE EXTINGUISHED.
WOWZA!

TEDDY!
HM?

HELP ME THINK OF A GOOD APRIL FOOL'S JOKE TO PLAY ON FRANCIS!

I REALLY WANT TO NAIL HIM!

HOW 'BOUT A GOOD OL' FASHIONED SNARE TRAP?
OOH! I LIKE IT!

WE'LL SET IT UP BEHIND THE GARAGE, AND THEN YOU CAN LURE HIM OVER HERE!
HEH HEH

? ?
SNAP!
ZIP!

WA HA HA HA HA HA HA!

GREAT JOB, TEDDY! HE DIDN'T SUSPECT A...

SNAP!

NEXT YEAR, WE'RE TEAMING UP AGAINST HIM.
AGREED.
KLIK!

BEFORE I HAND OUT THE UNIFORMS, GANG, HOW ABOUT A HAND FOR OUR NEW SPONSOR, **CRESSLY'S BAKERY**!!
CLAP CLAP
CLAP CLAP
CLAP CLAP
CLAP CLAP

THE CRESSLY FAMILY HAS OFFERED TO PROVIDE FRESH-BAKED SNACKS AFTER EVERY GAME... WIN OR LOSE!
YAAY!
WOO HOO!
COACH

COACH
SNIFF!

YOU OKAY, CHAD?
THIS IS THE HAPPIEST DAY OF MY LIFE.
COACH
Peirce

OKAY, EVERYONE, TIME TO HAND OUT THE UNIFORMS!
COACH

HERE YOU GO, NATE! NUMBER EIGHT!
WOW! THEY'VE GOT OUR NAMES ON THE BACK!
WRIGHT
8

WHAT DO THEY SAY ON THE FRONT?... "CRESSLY'S BAKERY"?
THEY SAY...

GAWK!
Peirce

CREAM PUFFS??
WRIGHT 8

FRANCIS! OUR UNIFORMS SAY CREAM PUFFS!
WELL, IT MAKES SENSE, RIGHT? OUR SPONSOR IS A BAKERY!

BUT... HMM... THEN AGAIN... I JUST THOUGHT OF SOMETHING.

DOESN'T IT MAKE US SOUND A TEENSY BIT WIMPY?
YES!

CREAM PUFFS? THAT'S OUR NAME? THE **CREAM PUFFS**?
WHAT'S WRONG WITH CREAM PUFFS? THEY'RE YUMMY!
CREAM

BUT A CREAM PUFF IS WHAT YOU CALL SOMEBODY WHO'S... LIKE... A **WUSS**! A **WEAKLING**!
OHHH... I GET IT.
CREAM PUFFS

YOU THINK IT MAKES US SOUND LIKE POPOVERS.
CREAM

THAT'S **PUSH**-OVERS, CHAD.
THEY MAKE PUSHOVERS **TOO**? **SWEET**!
POPE
7
CREAM

HEY, KIM, HERE'S A MESSAGE FOR YOUR PARENTS: THANKS FOR **NOTHING**!
CREAM PUFFS

WHEN THEIR BAKERY BECAME OUR SPONSOR, I DIDN'T KNOW THEY WERE GOING TO CALL US THE **CREAM PUFFS**!

CREAM PUFFS

WHAT A STUPID NAME! WHAT A...
YOUR EARS TURN RED WHEN YOU GET MAD. THAT'S ADORABLE.

URK!
NOW TELL ME SOMETHING ABOUT **ME** THAT'S ADORABLE.

I KNOW OUR NAME'S NOT EXACTLY IN-TIMIDATING, GANG, BUT MAYBE WE CAN FLIP THAT AROUND!
HUH?
WHAT'S THAT MEAN?
COACH

WELL, WHAT IF WE'RE REALLY **GOOD**? A POWERHOUSE TEAM CALLED THE "CREAM PUFFS" COULD BE KIND OF **IRONIC**!

LIKE IF PEOPLE CALLED YOU "CURLY" EVEN THOUGH YOU'RE BALD?
COACH

JUST FOR THE RECORD: I'M NOT BALD, I SHAVE MY HEAD.
MY DAD CALLS THAT A "PRE-EMPTIVE STRIKE."
COACH

MY LIFE IS RUINED.
HM? WHY'S THAT, BUD?

MY BASEBALL TEAM! WE'RE SPONSORED BY CRESSLY'S BAKERY, AND YOU KNOW WHAT THEY PUT ON OUR UNIFORMS?

NOT "CRESSLY'S BAKERY"?
NO! "CREAM PUFFS"! RIGHT ACROSS OUR CHESTS IT SAYS "CREAM PUFFS"!

IS THAT THE WORST NAME EVER OR WHAT? WE'RE GOING TO BE A LAUGHINGSTOCK!

ALL THE OTHER TEAMS HAVE REAL NAMES LIKE "AL'S AUTO GLASS" AND "CYCLE CITY"! BUT NOT US!

IT'S A TOTAL NIGHT-MARE.
WELL, THINK OF IT THIS WAY:

YOU'RE YOUNG, YOU'RE HEALTHY, AND THE BIGGEST PROBLEM YOU'VE GOT IS THE NAME OF YOUR BALL TEAM!

GRAMPS IS MINIMIZING MY SUFFER-ING AGAIN.
AW, TOO BAD, SWEETIE. HAVE A COOKIE.
Peirce

OPENING DAY, BOYS! OPENING DAY!
LET'S GO GET 'EM!

IS IT TRUE?... IT IS!!
! !

GUYS! THEY REALLY ARE CALLED THE CREAM PUFFS!

HA HA HA HA HA HA
I'M ACTUALLY FEELING NOSTALGIC FOR THE SEASON WE WERE SPONSORED BY "CHEZ LINDA."
Peirce

HEY, CREAM PUFFS! BEFORE WE START THE GAME, MAYBE WE SHOULD MAKE A TRADE!
A TRADE?

YEAH, THERE'S A KID ON OUR TEAM WHO SHOULD BE ON YOURS!
YEAH? WHY'S THAT?

HE'S DANISH!

WA HA HA HA HA HA HA HA H
I'M SERIOUSLY THINKING OF SWITCHING TO LACROSSE.
Peirce

THIS IS GOING TO GET OLD REALLY FAST.
WHAT IS?

OTHER TEAMS **RANKING ON US** FOR BEING CALLED THE **CREAM PUFFS**! I DON'T KNOW HOW MANY **PASTRY JOKES** I CAN **TAKE**!

SMACK!

NICE BUNS.

SAY, COACH, COULD I HAVE A QUICK WORD BEFORE WE GET STARTED?
SURE.

I'D APPRECIATE IT IF YOUR KIDS STOPPED RIDICULING OUR TEAM'S NAME. THEY'VE BEEN GIVING MY KIDS QUITE AN EARFUL DURING WARM-UPS.

IF YOUR KIDS DON'T LIKE IT, TELL 'EM TO SIGN UP FOR BALLET LESSONS.

LET'S CREAM THESE GUYS.

OKAY, GANG, LET'S PLAY BALL! AND IF THE OTHER TEAM WANTS TO MAKE FUN OF OUR NAME, **LET** 'EM!
CLAP
CLAP
CLAP

WE'LL SHOW 'EM THAT A CREAM PUFF MAY BE... UH... FLAKY ON THE **OUTSIDE**, BUT... IT'S... UM... HM... IT'S...
COACH

COACH
...SOFT AND SWEET ON THE INSIDE?

TELL YOU WHAT, JUST TAKE THE FIELD.
EPIC FAIL ON THE PRE-GAME PEP TALK, COACH.
COAC
Peirce

THAT'S IT! BALL-GAME OVER!
SNAG!

GOOD GAME, CHAD! GOOD GAME, TEDDY! GOOD GAME, FRANCIS!

UH...GOOD GAME, KIM.

HIGH FIVES ARE SO UNROMANTIC.
...AND UN-PAINFUL.
Peirce

LET'S GO, CREAM PUFFS!
PARENT?

UH-HUH. YOU?
GRAND-PARENT.

WHICH ONE'S YOURS?
KIM. SHE'S THE ONLY GIRL ON THE TEAM.

MINE'S NATE. NUMBER EIGHT.
AH! SO THAT'S NATE!

MY GRANDDAUGHTER SPEAKS MIGHTY HIGHLY OF YOUR SON!
WELL, THAT'S VERY NICE! THANK YOU!

YUP! EVER SINCE BASEBALL SEASON STARTED, ALL SHE TALKS ABOUT IS NATE, NATE, NATE!

JUST BETWEEN YOU AND ME, I THINK SHE HAS QUITE A CRUSH ON YOUR YOUNG MAN!

YOU'RE CHOKING ME.
IT'S CALLED "TEAM BONDING."

NOTHING EVER HAPPENS IN THIS DUMP.
WHAT WOULD YOU LIKE TO HAPPEN?

ANYTHING! ANYTHING TO BREAK UP THE MONOTONY OF DOING THE EXACT SAME THING DAY AFTER DAY AFTER...

POP QUIZ, PEOPLE.
!

SHE HEARD YOU.
HOW COME WE NEVER HAVE ANY POP FIELD TRIPS?
Peirce

WAIT! MRS. GODFREY, YOU CAN'T GIVE US A POP QUIZ! IT'S NOT **FAIR**!

I MEAN, WE DON'T EVEN KNOW WHAT YOU'RE **QUIZZING** US ON! RIGHT, GANG? RIGHT?

WHEN CLASS ENDED YESTERDAY, PEOPLE, WHAT DID I **SPECIFICALLY** ASK YOU TO READ AND REVIEW?

CHAPTER 6, QUESTIONS 12-28!
I HATE THEM ALL.
Peirce

A POP QUIZ! WHAT A DIRTY TRICK THAT WAS!
I AM NOT UNDERSTAND WHY IS IT CALLED A POP QUIZ.

BECAUSE THEY POP IT ON YOU, ARTUR! POP MEANS THE ELEMENT OF SURPRISE! IT'S LIKE: HERE'S A QUIZ! POP!

ONE TIME I GOT A DILL PICKLE STUCK UP MY NOSE, AND WHEN MY GRAM PULLED IT OUT, IT MADE A REALLY LOUD POP!

peirce
NOW I AM NOT UNDERSTAND WHY CHAD PUT A DILL PICKLE INSIDE HIS NOSE.
I WAS EXPERI-MENTING!

I DON'T SEE THE POINT OF POP QUIZZES. HOW AM I SUPPOSED TO KNOW THE ANSWERS TO SOME-THING I DIDN'T **STUDY** FOR?
WHY DIDN'T YOU STUDY?

BECAUSE I DIDN'T KNOW WE WERE GOING TO HAVE A **QUIZ**, FRANCIS!
YOU SHOULD **ALWAYS** EXPECT A QUIZ! EVERY DAY!

PREPARATION IS THE KEY! IF YOU PREPARE FOR **ANYTHING**, THEN NOTHING WILL CATCH YOU OFF-GUARD!

FIVE SECONDS LATER...
ALMOST NOTHING.
GOTCHA!
Peirce

NATE, YOUR PERFORMANCE ON YESTERDAY'S QUIZ WAS, TO BE CHARITABLE, **DISMAL**.

FOR EXAMPLE, QUESTION NUMBER THREE ASKED: WHO WAS THOMAS PAINE?

THE CORRECT RESPONSE WOULD HAVE BEEN THAT HE WAS ONE OF THE FOUNDING FATHERS AND THE AUTHOR OF "COMMON SENSE."...

... **NOT** A "GRAMMY-WINNING RAPPER WHO IS CHANGING THE FACE OF HIP-HOP"!
SO THEY'RE BOTH REVOLUTIONARIES.
Peirce

ALL THIS JUNK THEY TEACH US IN SCHOOL IS A WASTE OF TIME! WHEN ARE WE EVER GOING TO **USE** THIS STUFF?

THEY SHOULD TEACH US **REAL-LIFE** SKILLS, LIKE HOW TO TIE KNOTS, OR HOW TO FIX A FLAT TIRE!
WHY SHOULD **SCHOOLS** DO THAT?
WRIGHT

STUFF LIKE THAT IS WHAT **PARENTS** ARE SUPPOSED TO TEACH YOU!

...AND NOW, BACK TO "DANCE MOMS."
CRUNCH
CRUNCH
RUNCH
RIIIIIGHT.
peirce

Big Nate is distributed internationally by Universal Uclick.

Andrews McMeel Publishing
a division of Andrews McMeel Universal
1130 Walnut Street, Kansas City, Missouri 64106

www.andrewsmcmeel.com

16 17 18 19 20 SDB 10 9 8 7 6 5 4 3 2 1

ISBN: 978-1-4494-6227-7

Library of Congress Control Number: 2015953083

Made by:
Shenzhen Donnelley Printing Company Ltd.
Address and location of manufacturer:
No. 47, Wuhe Nan Road, Bantian Ind. Zone,
Shenzhen China, 518129
1st Printing—12/7/15

These strips appeared in newspapers from October 31, 2011, through April 21, 2012.

Big Nate can be viewed on the Internet at www.gocomics.com/big_nate

Check out these and other books at ampkids.com

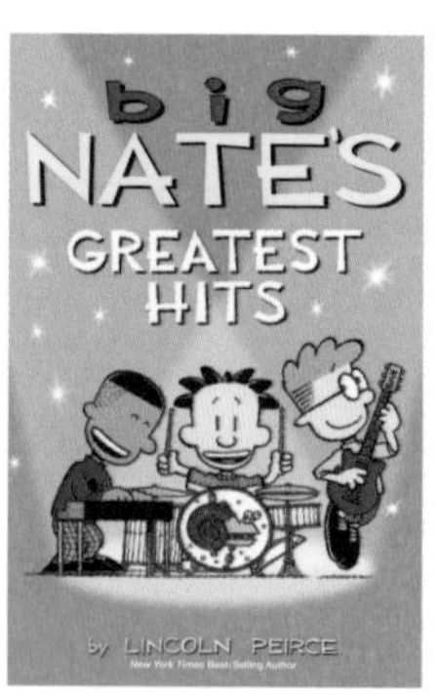

Also available:
Teaching and activity guides for each title.
AMP! Comics for Kids books make reading FUN!